P9-EEL-482

Disney
FAIRIES

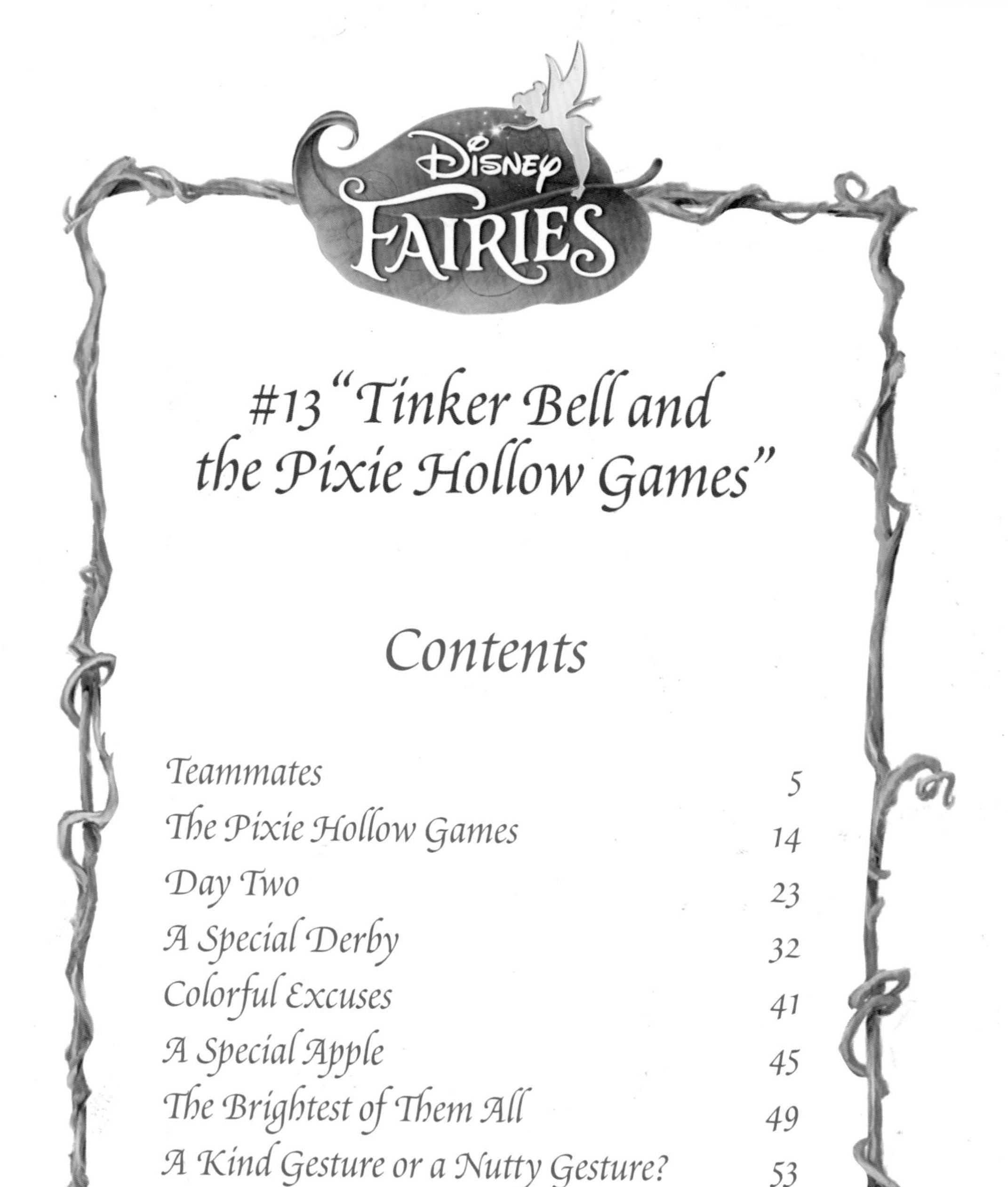

#13 "Tinker Bell and the Pixie Hollow Games"

Contents

PAPERCUTZ™
NEW YORK

"Teammates," "The Pixie Hollow Games,"
"Day Two," and "A Special Derby"
Concept and Script: Tea Orsi
Revised Captions: Cortney Faye Powell
Layout: Sara Storino
Pencils: Marino Gentile
Inks: Roberta Zanotta
Color: Studio Kawaii
Letters: Janice Chiang
Page 5, 14, & 23 art:
Concept: Tea Orsi
Pencils & Inks: Sara Storino & Marino Gentile
Color: Andrea Cagol
Page 32 art:
Concept: Tea Orsi
Pencils and Inks: Marino Gentile
Color: Mara Damiani

"Colorful Excuses"
Concept and Script: Tea Orsi
Revised Dialogue: Cortney Faye Powell
Layout, Pencils, & Inks: Monica Catalano
Color: Studio Kawaii
Letters: Janice Chiang

"A Special Apple'
Concept and Script: Tea Orsi
Revised Dialogue: Cortney Faye Powell
Layout, Pencils, & Inks: Monica Catalano
Color: Studio Kawaii
Letters: Janice Chiang

"The Brightest of Them All"
Concept and Script: Tea Orsi
Revised Dialogue: Cortney Faye Powell
Layout & Pencils: Manuela Razzi
Inks: Roberta Zanotta
Color: Studio Kawaii
Letters: Janice Chiang

"A Kind Gesture or a Nutty Gesture?"
Concept and Script: Tea Orsi
Revised Dialogue: Cortney Faye Powell
Layout, Pencils, & Inks: Monica Catalano
Color: Studio Kawaii
Letters: Janice Chiang

Production – Dawn K. Guzzo
Special Thanks – Shiho Tilley and John Tanzer
Production Coordinator – Beth Scorzato
Associate Editor – Michael Petranek
Jim Salicrup
Editor-in-Chief

ISBN: 978-1-59707-446-9 paperback edition
ISBN: 978-1-59707-447-6 hardcover edition

Printed in China
December 2013 by Asia One Printing LTD
13/F Asia One Tower
8 Fung Yip St., Chaiwan
Hong Kong

Papercutz books may be purchased for business or promotional use.
For information on bulk purchases please contact
Macmillan Corporate and Premium Sales Department at
(800) 221-7945 x5442.

Distributed by Macmillan
First Papercutz Printing

HEY, TINK, REMEMBER THAT TIME I ACCIDENTALLY SPLATTERED MUD ON ROSETTA?
LIKE THIS...
BZZT
BZZT
THIS TIME YOU DID THAT ON PURPOSE!
HOW COULD WE POSSIBLY FORGET...

TEAMMATES

TONIGHT, MARKS THE BEGINNING OF THE *PIXIE HOLLOW GAMES!*
A TRADITION IN WHICH ALL THE DIFFERENT TALENT FAIRIES COMPETE AGAINST ONE ANOTHER OVER THE COURSE OF THREE DAYS.
ALL THE FAIRIES ARE NOW BUSY DECORATING THE ARENA BUILT AT THE FOOT OF THE PIXIE DUST TREE.
AND ***ROSETTA*** AND ***SILVERMIST*** TAKE GREAT CARE IN THE DECORATION PROCESS TO HONOR THE TRADITION OF THE COMPETITION, MAKING SURE EVERYTHING IS PERFECT...
RIGHT HERE WILL BE JUST DIVINE, THANK YOU!

ALL IT TAKES IS A PINCH OF PIXIE DUST AND...
LOOKIN' GOOD, ROSETTA!
WELL...
THERE'S A REASON I'M IN CHARGE OF BEAUTIFICATION, TINKER BELL!
IRIDESSA AND FAWN ARE PLEASED WITH THE PREPARATIONS AS WELL.
EVERYTHING LOOKS GREAT, RO!
ROSETTA'S GREATEST SKILL AS A GARDEN FAIRY, IS MAKING THINGS PRETTY, AND THAT JOB SEEMS TO BE COMPLETE FOR THE GAMES. NOW SHE CAN RELAX AND WATCH FROM AFAR...

BUT SUDDENLY...
VIDIA!
WHOOSH
HEY, SEE THERE, WHO'S MISS MUDPIE?

VIDIA NOTICES CHLOE, A NEWLY ARRIVED GARDEN FAIRY, WHO DEFINITELY DOESN'T SEEM MUCH LIKE ROSETTA...
HUT-HUT-HUT-HUT-HUT!
NOW, WHAT IN NEVER LAND...?!

CHLOE, DON'T TRAMPLE THE FLOWERS!
HUH?! WHOA!

WHEW! THE DECORATIONS ARE SAFE AND SOUND, BUT...
OOOH!

UH-OH! ROSETTA HATES MUD...
OH, MY GOODNESS, ROSETTA! I'M SO SORRY!
SPLOTCH

DIRT! GET IT OFF, GET IT OFF!
RO! ARE YOU OKAY?
YOU'RE AFRAID OF DIRT, AND YOU'RE A *GARDEN* FAIRY?

I LOVE YOUR ROCK! UM... WHAT ARE YOU DOING WITH IT?
OH... I'M *TRAINING!*

TRAINING?
FOR THE *PIXIE HOLLOW GAMES,* OF COURSE!

I'VE BEEN STUDYING ALL KINDS OF *STRATEGIES* AND WORKING REALLY HARD AT--
WAIT, WAIT, WAIT!

YOU ACTUALLY *WANT* TO BE ON THE GARDEN FAIRY TEAM?
WELL, YEAH... DON'T YOU?!

TSK! NEW ARRIVAL!
WHY? AM I THE ONLY ONE WHO WANTS TO BE ON THE TEAM?

TINK AND THE GIRLS KNOW WHY BUT DON'T DARE TO SAY ANYTHING...

ONLY ROSETTA DOES...
I'LL TELL YOU WHY!
BECAUSE WE STINK!
?!
AH, YES! THE HISTORY OF THE GAMES IS FILLED WITH TALES OF GARDEN FAIRY FAILURE!
WE'VE NEVER EVEN COME CLOSE TO WINNIN'!
WELL, WHY CAN'T GARDEN FAIRIES BE AS GOOD AS EVERYONE ELSE?

THIS COULD BE THE YEAR THE LOSING STREAK ENDS! WE WOULD MAKE HISTORY!
SWEETPEA...

WE BRING BEAUTY TO THE WORLD! THAT'S WHAT WE'RE GOOD AT!

BUT THE NEW ARRIVAL, CHLOE, DOESN'T BUY IN TO THAT!
NO! I FOR ONE, THINK WE CAN WIN!

WE CAN WIN, IF NO ONE ELSE SHOWS UP!

FERN INTERRUPTS, AS IT IS TIME TO PICK THE GARDEN FAIRY TEAM!
GATHER 'ROUND, GARDEN FAIRIES!

THE FAIRIES GATHER AROUND HER, NONE TOO EAGER TO BE CHOSEN. WELL EXCEPT ONE...
CHLOE HAS ALREADY VOLUNTEERED!
DIG DOWN DEEP AND BREAK THE STREAK!

THE FAIRIES WATCH WITH WORRIED ANTICIPATION... EXCEPT ROSETTA, WHO DOESN'T SEEM CONCERNED...
OOOKAY... BUT WE NEED TO PICK HER TEAM-MATE!
PLEASE DON'T LET IT BE ME...

ROSETTA?!

TINK AND THE OTHERS OVERHEAR THE NAME AND ARE STUNNED...
GASP!

BUT NOT AS STUNNED AS ROSETTA IS... WHO WAS JUST ABOUT TO TAKE HER AFTERNOON BEAUTY NAP!
NO, NO, NO... THERE MUST BE SOME MISTAKE!
SEE, THAT SAYS ROSEEEETA!
IT'S YOU!
Rosetta
ROSETTA'S ALWAYS WEASELED OUT OF THE GAMES, BUT NOW SHE HAS NO CHOICE!
YOURS IS THE ONLY NAME IN THERE! IT'S YOUR TURN!
WHAT?!
Rosetta
CHLOE WASN'T THRILLED ABOUT ROSETTA BEING PICKED EITHER, BUT...
UGH! FINE... FINE... I'LL DO IT!
ALL RIGHT, SO...

?!
LET'S GO BRING HOME THAT TROPHY!
WILL ROSETTA AND CHLOE MANAGE TO CHANGE THE HISTORY OF THE GAMES? A MAGICAL ADVENTURE IS ABOUT TO BEGIN...
?!
TO BE CONTINUED...

IF THE PIXIE HOLLOW GAMES WERE A FASHION CONTEST-- YOU'D WIN, ROSETTA!
FINALLY-- CHLOE, WE AGREE!

THE PIXIE HOLLOW GAMES

THE FIRST TEAMS ENTER THE ARENA...
THE FAST-FLYING FAIRIES...
THE ANIMAL FAIRIES...
THE LIGHT FAIRIES AND THE WATER FAIRIES!

TINKER BELL AND FAIRY MARY ARE THE TINKER TEAM!

THE DUST- KEEPER TEAM IS THE NEXT TO ARRIVE! EACH TEAM IN SPECIAL UNIFORMS...
HEE, HEE!

EXCEPT THE GARDEN FAIRIES...
HONEYDEW, WE'RE NOT GONNA LAST MORE THAN ONE EVENT!
ROSETTA, YOU DO KNOW WE'RE COMPETING, NOT SPECTATING, RIGHT?
IF I'M GONNA LOOK BAD, I'M NOT GONNA LOOK BAD!
DON'T WORRY! WE'LL DO A MAKEOVER ON YOU LATER!
!
RUMBLE AND GLIMMER, THE STORM FAIRIES, MAKE THEIR GRAND ENTRANCE...
WHERE THERE'S LIGHTNING...
THERE'S THUNDER!
BOOM

THEY'RE GOING FOR A RECORD FIFTH STRAIGHT CHAMPIONSHIP RING AND EVERYONE CHEERS FOR THEM!

ALL THE ATHLETES ARE READY!
FIREWORKS FILL THE SKY...
AND QUEEN CLARION PRESIDES OVER THE OPENING CEREMONIES...
BOOM
GOOD LUCK TO ALL OUR COMPETITORS... AND MAY THE BEST TEAM WIN!
HOORAY!
YAY!

THE FIRST EVENT BEGINS: *LEAPFROGGING!*
KABLAM

ALL THE TEAMS TAKE OFF... EXCEPT ONE...
ROSETTA, YOU ACTUALLY HAVE TO SIT ON THE FROG!
I'M NOT PUTTING MY *PETUNIA* ON THAT SLIMY THING!

FINALLY ROSETTA SEEMS TO SIT DOWN BUT...

AAAHHH!

SHE CAN'T CONTROL HER FROG, WHICH SWERVES AND BLOCKS THE TRACK BUT...
OUTTA MY WAY!
UGH!
THE OTHER TEAMS MANAGE TO PASS!

EXCEPT THE HEALING TALENT FAIRIES WHO AREN'T DOING VERY WELL, EITHER.
SNAP
DUE TO ROSETTA'S ACCIDENT, THE ANIMAL FAIRIES PULL IN FRONT OF THE STORM FAIRIES TO WIN THE FIRST EVENT.
ALL RIGHT!
LATER, OUR HEROINES ALSO REACH THE FINISH LINE...
UGH! OH, GROSS!

GASP!
I KNEW YOU COULD DO IT!

ROSETTA AND CHLOE ARE IN LAST PLACE, BUT THEY'RE STILL IN IT!
HA HA! THIS IS GREAT!
SINCE THE HEALING TALENT FAIRIES DIDN'T FINISH, YOU GUYS MOVE ON TO THE NEXT EVENT!

RO ISN'T THRILLED AND NEITHER IS RUMBLE...
IF IT WASN'T FOR THOSE GARDEN FAIRIES WE'D BE IN FIRST PLACE RIGHT NOW!

BUT NOW IT'S TIME TO GET SOME REST...
JUST WAIT UNTIL TOMORROW. THAT'S WHEN WE'LL MAKE OUR MOVE!
WE'RE IN LAST PLACE! IT'S JUST A MATTER OF TIME TILL WE...
THE OTHER GARDEN FAIRIES ARE EXCITED ABOUT THEIR TEAM'S PERFORMANCE...
DO YOU REALIZE WHAT YOU HAVE DONE?
YOU MADE IT FARTHER THAN ANY GARDEN FAIRY TEAM IN HISTORY!

TO BE CONTINUED...

HONEY, THIS PARTICULAR CHALLENGE HAS TURNED INTO A *TEMPEST IN A TEACUP!*
HA! JUST HOLD ON!

THE SECOND DAY

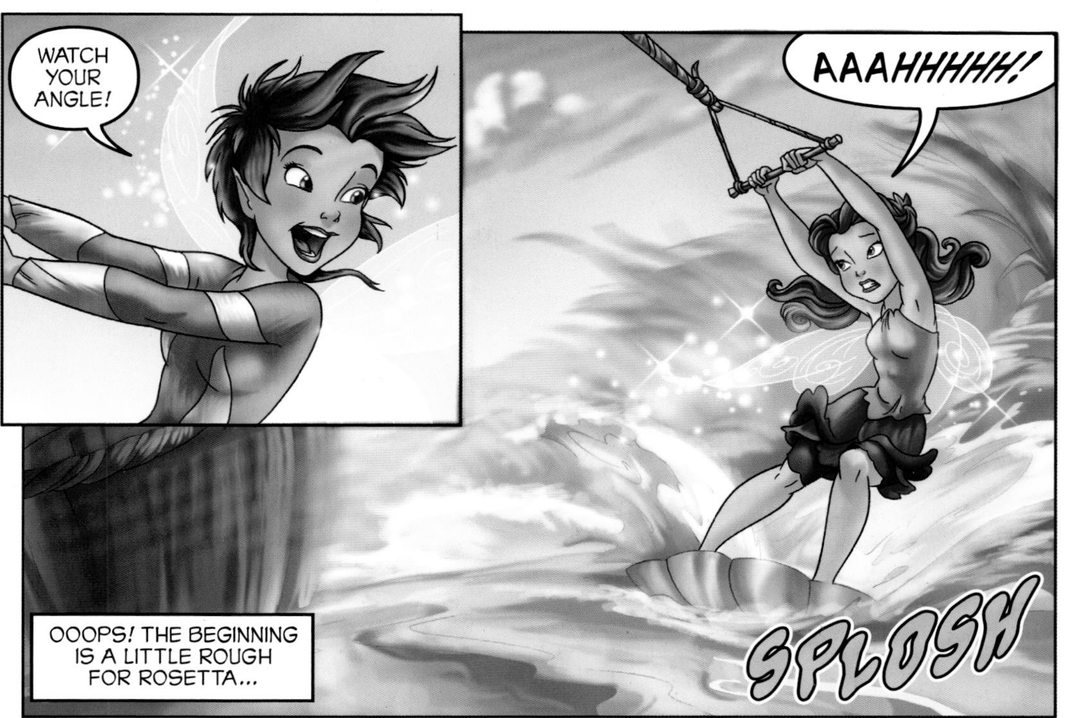
WATCH YOUR ANGLE!
AAAHHHHH!
OOOPS! THE BEGINNING IS A LITTLE ROUGH FOR ROSETTA...
SPLOSH

BUT WITH A BIT OF TEAM WORK...
AND A DETERMINATION NOT TO RUIN HER OUTFIT...
CAREFUL ON THE EDGE CHANGE...
YEAH, YOU GOT IT!
WOOOSH
SPLOSH
ROSETTA DOES REALLY WELL AND THE GARDEN FAIRY TEAM IS STILL IN THE GAME!

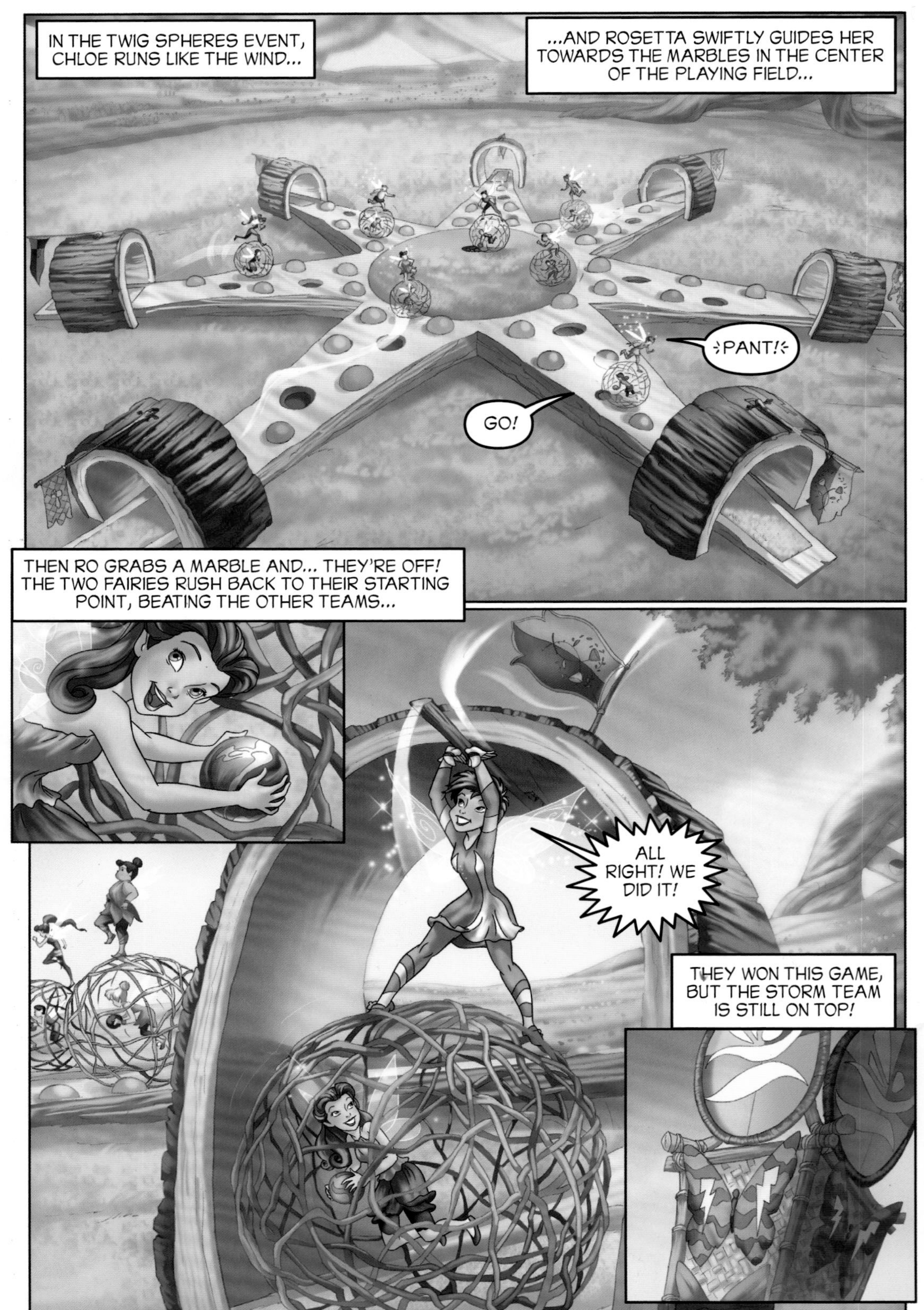
IN THE TWIG SPHERES EVENT, CHLOE RUNS LIKE THE WIND...
...AND ROSETTA SWIFTLY GUIDES HER TOWARDS THE MARBLES IN THE CENTER OF THE PLAYING FIELD...
PANT!
GO!
THEN RO GRABS A MARBLE AND... THEY'RE OFF! THE TWO FAIRIES RUSH BACK TO THEIR STARTING POINT, BEATING THE OTHER TEAMS...
ALL RIGHT! WE DID IT!
THEY WON THIS GAME, BUT THE STORM TEAM IS STILL ON TOP!

NEXT IS THE MOUSE POLO MATCH, WHERE THE GARDEN FAIRIES ADVANCE EVEN FURTHER! YOU WOULD THINK ROSETTA WAS BORN TO RIDE A MOUSE!
WOOOM
...AND WITH SOME FANTASTIC TEAMWORK, ROSETTA SCORES THE WINNING GOAL!
THE CROWD GOES WILD!
GREAT JOB!
GO ROSETTA!

AND EVEN GLIMMER IS IMPRESSED, TO RO'S GREAT SURPRISE...
GOOD GAME!
THANK YOU!

BUT RUMBLE SNAPS AT HER...
WHY DON'T YOU WORRY ABOUT YOUR OWN GAME?
?!

NOW THE GARDEN FAIRY TEAM IS DETERMINED TO WIN THE DAY'S LAST EVENT: THE TEACUP CHALLENGE!
IN THE TUNNEL, CHLOE AND RO EVEN PASS GLIMMER AND RUMBLE!

AND THEY'RE THE FIRST ONES TO COME OUT, WHERE THEY FACE THE LAST OBSTACLE BETWEEN THEM AND THE FINISH LINE: THE SLIDE COVERED IN SLUG SLIME!
CHLOE DOESN'T WASTE ANY TIME. SHE DIVES RIGHT DOWN THE CHUTE...
AND SHE CROSSES THE FINISH LINE FIRST...
YES! WE DID IT! WE'RE IN FIRST PLACE, RO!
YAAAAY!
BUT THEN SHE REALIZES SHE'S ALONE!
RO?!

UH-OH, ROSETTA DOESN'T WANT TO GET DIRTY...
COME ON, IT'S FASTER IF YOU GET IN THE SLIME!
NO, NO! I'LL JUST MEET YOU DOWN THERE...

GET OUT OF MY WAY!
SPLISH
SPLOSH
MEANWHILE THE STORM FAIRIES ARRIVE AND ZOOM DOWN, WINNING THE EVENT...

IN NO TIME, THE OTHER TEAMS ALSO MOVE OUT AHEAD, BUT RO AND CHLOE ARE STILL THERE.
IF WE DON'T FINISH *TOGETHER* IT DOESN'T COUNT!
CHLOE, I WANT TO, BUT I JUST CAN'T DO IT!
OH.

AND ANYWAY, IT'S TOO LATE!
OOH! *BAD LUCK* FOR THE GARDEN FAIRIES!
OUR HEROINES ARE STILL IN THE FINAL EVENT, BUT NO ONE HAS EVER WON IT FROM LAST PLACE!

IN THE STANDS, TINK AND THE OTHERS ARE FEELING BAD FOR ROSETTA AND CHLOE...
WHAT HAPPENED?
THEY WERE DOING SO WELL!

BUT THERE'S SOMEONE WHO FINDS IT ALL REALLY FUNNY...
HA HA HA!
EWW, EWW!
OH, YOU REALLY MADE RUMBLE LAUGH!

ALL THAT BUMBLIN' AND STUMBLIN' JUST SO YOU WOULDN'T GET DIRTY?!
OF ALL THE GARDEN FAIRY FAILURES, THIS HAS GOT TO BE THE MOST HUMILIATING OF ALL TIME!

HEY, WHAT'S YOUR POINT?
WELL, MY POINT IS GARDEN FAIRIES SHOULD JUST STICK TO BEING PRETTY!

THAT'S WHAT YOU ARE GOOD AT!
!

HEY, BUT THAT'S WHAT YOU'VE BEEN DOING!
HUH?!

CHLOE, I...
DON'T BLAME YOURSELF. YOU DID EVERYTHING YOU COULD!
WELL, I--

FINALLY RUMBLE LEAVES...
UH-UH!
OH!

BUT, NO! RO KNOWS SHE DIDN'T...
GUESS I'LL GET CLEANED-UP FOR THE FINAL EVENT TOMORROW...
WE'RE GONNA LOOK BAD, WE DON'T WANT TO LOOK BAD, YOU KNOW.
SIGH!
BUT MAYBE IT'S NOT TOO LATE...
TO BE CONTINUED...

GET READY FOR THE WACKIEST RACE EVER!

A SPECIAL DERBY
THE FINAL DAY OF THE GAMES IS HERE! AND THE REMAINING TEAMS ARE PREPARING VIGOROUSLY FOR THEIR ULTIMATE CHALLENGE, WHICH IS TO COMPETE IN A PIXIE CART DERBY ABOARD THEIR FANTASTIC RACING CARTS!
CLANG
BANG
SQUEAK
AS THE TINKER FAIRIES ARE MAKING SOME LAST-MINUTE ADJUSTMENTS...
...CHLOE IS STILL WAITING FOR ROSETTA TO MAKE AN APPEARANCE. AFTER YESTERDAY'S DOWNFALL, SHE IS ALMOST OUT OF HOPE...
... UNTIL...
ROSETTA?!

IS THAT YOU?
CHLOE, I OWE YOU AN APOLOGY...

YOU DIDN'T NEED A MAKEOVER! I DID!

I FINISHED THE MODIFICATIONS WE ST-- WHOA, RO, YOU LOOK AMAZING!
YOU GUYS MODIFIED THE CART?!

I STUDIED THE DERBY AND I HAVE A PLAN TO WIN THIS WHOLE THING!
NOW ARE YOU READY TO DIG DOWN DEEP?
OH, YEAH... AND BREAK THE STREAK!

CLANK AND BOBBLE PRESENT THE RACE: THERE ARE THREE SHORTCUTS, EACH MORE DIFFICULT THAN THE LAST...
...THE TEAMS CAN CHOOSE WHETHER TO TAKE THEM OR CONTINUE ALONG THE SAFEST PATH...
THIS IS IT, FAIRY FANS: THE FINAL *EVENT!* THERE ARE ONLY *THREE* CHANCES TO PASS...
"THE *JUMP...*"
"...THE POND..."
"...AND *MUDSLIDE MOUNTAIN!*"
THE TEAMS ARE ON THE STARTING LINE...
AND RO AND CHLOE ARE ONCE AGAIN, DETERMINED TO WIN!

GO! THE PIXIE CART DERBY BEGINS...
SWISSSSH
THE FAST-FLYING TEAM TRIES THE JUMP, BUT UNFORTUNATELY THEY MAKE A BAD LANDING AND ARE OUT OF THE GAMES...
WHOAAA!
CRASH

THEN THE DUST-KEEPER TEAM ATTEMPTS THE SECOND SHORTCUT, BUT IT DOESN'T GO WELL...
SPLISH
SPLOSH

RUMBLE AND GLIMMER ARE STILL IN THE LEAD AND PULL EVEN FARTHER AHEAD...
VROOM

BUT, AS SHE SAID, RO HAS A PLAN TO PASS THE STORM FAIRIES...
JUST PUT THESE ON AND PULL THE LEVER WHEN I SAY!
WOW! THEY EVEN MATCH OUR OUTFITS!
THEY TAKE THE MUDSLIDE MOUNTAIN SHORTCUT. THIS IS THEIR LAST CHANCE TO PASS, BUT NO TEAM HAS EVER MADE IT OVER BEFORE...
SPLOSH
NOW!
SPLASH
FINALLY CHLOE PULLS THE LEVER...
SCREEEECH
AND THE WHEELS TRANSFORM...
SPROING
NOW THE GARDEN FAIRY TEAM CAN ZOOM UP THE MOUNTAIN...
SPLOSH
VRRRR
IT'S TIME TO GET *DIRTY!*
SPLASH

ONCE THEY'RE AT THE TOP, THE CART TURNS INTO A TOBOGGAN, MAKING THEIR DESCENT EVEN FASTER THAN THEIR CLIMB...

THE GARDEN FAIRIES GET BACK ON THE TRACK PASSING THE STORM FAIRY TEAM AND PULLING OUT IN FRONT!

THE TWO CARTS GO INTO THE TUNNEL, BUT RUMBLE ISN'T ABOUT TO LET THEM BEAT HIM...

AND, IN A SNEAKY MOVE, HE USES GLIMMER'S LIGHTNING...

RUMBLE'S CHEATING WORKS AND HE CROSSES THE FINISH LINE FIRST...

YESSSS!

BUT RO AND CHLOE DON'T GIVE UP...
LET'S CROSS THAT FINISH LINE!
LET'S DO IT!

AND THEY COMPLETE THE RACE ANYWAY, PUSHING THEIR CART OVER THE FINISH LINE...
CREAK
CREAK

QUEEN CLARION ANNOUNCES THE FINAL OUTCOME AND SURPRISES EVERYONE...
AND THE WINNERS OF THE *PIXIE HOLLOW GAMES* ARE... THE *GARDEN FAIRIES!*
BUT RUMBLE CROSSED THE FINISH LINE FIRST!

YES, RUMBLE DID... BUT TEAMMATES MUST FINISH *TOGETHER!*
HUH?!

TURNS OUT GLIMMER WAS NOT WITH RUMBLE!

AH, YES! RO AND CHLOE REALLY DESERVED TO WIN AND ARE PROUD TO BE GARDEN FAIRIES!
WE DID IT! WE DID IT! WE DID IT! **WE BROKE THE STREAK!**

FINALLY, THE GARDEN FAIRIES CAN CELEBRATE THEIR FIRST TRIUMPH WITH THEIR FRIENDS OF ALL TALENTS...
IN THE HISTORY OF THE GAMES, THERE'S NEVER BEEN A MORE SPECIAL VICTORY, AND FOR ROSETTA AND CHLOE, THE BIGGEST PRIZE IS THEIR WONDERFUL NEW FRIENDSHIP!
HOORAY!
HOORAY FOR RO AND CHLOE!

COLORFUL EXCUSES
IN SPRINGTIME SQUARE, SOME FAIRIES ARE HAVING TOO MUCH FUN--ON A SLIP 'N' SLIDE RAINBOW!?
HA, HA!
WHEEE!
SWISHHH
SWISHHH

LOOK AT MEEEEEEE! AHHHH...

NOW THIS IS WHAT I CALL A FLITTERIFIC TIME! I HOPE WE DON'T GET CAUGHT.
ME, TOO! IRIDESSA WILL BE FURIOUS IF SHE SEES US SLIDING ON ONE OF HER RAINBOWS! HEE HEE.

DON'T WORRY! SHE WON'T NOTICE ANYTHI--
WHERE'S THE RAINBOW YOU WANT US TO ROLL UP, IRIDESSA?!
OOPS! WHY DID I SAY ANYTHING?!
LET'S HIDE, QUICK!
THE FAIRIES FLY OFF TO THE SIDE AND...
OH, THERE IT IS!
GASP!
I'VE NEVER SEEN A RAINBOW IN SUCH TERRIBLE SHAPE BEFORE!
HUH? OH, NO! WHO COULD'VE DONE THIS?!
UM... HI, GIRLS.

WHAT HAVE YOU FAIRIES BEEN UP TO? MAYBE YOU SAW WHO MADE SUCH A MESS OUT OF THIS BEAUTIFUL RAINBOW?
UM... WHO? US?
UM... WE WERE JUST HANGING WITH *LADY*.

IS THAT SO, *ROSETTA?* WELL, ANY IDEAS WHO COULD HAVE DONE THIS? LOOKS LIKE THEY HAD A LOT OF FUN, WHOEVER IT WAS...
SORRY, *SILVERMIST!* WE WERE ALL *PREOCCUPIED...*

YEAH, *REALLY PREOCCUPIED! HEE, HEE!*
OH?

HOW STRANGE!
VERY! CONSIDERING THAT THEY WERE RIGHT HERE...
UM... WE REALLY NEED TO GO NOW!
BUT THE MOMENT THEY TURN TO LEAVE...
GASP! WILL YOU LOOK AT THAT!
AHA! I KNEW IT!
HA,HA! SHOULD WE SAY SOMETHING... IT'S JUST TOO FUNNY.
AH, YES! IN THEIR RUSH, TINK, RO AND FAWN DIDN'T NOTICE A VERY COLORFUL DETAIL THE RAINBOW LEFT BEHIND...
THEY LOOK SO SILLY, I CAN'T BE MAD AT THEM! HA! HA!
I WONDER WHAT THEY'RE LAUGHING ABOUT...
THE END

A SPECIAL APPLE
ROSETTA'S SPRUCING UP SOME FLOWERS WHEN...
?!
THERE YOU GO! NOW YOU'RE ALL BRIGHT AND SHINY.
...SHE NOTICES CHLOE, A GARDEN FAIRY WHO WOULD RATHER PLAY IN THE MUD WITH WORMS THAN ACTUALLY GARDEN...
GASP! I DON'T BELIEVE MY FAIRY EYES!
ONE LAST TOUCH AND IT'LL BE PERFECT!
CHLOE! WHAT ARE YOU DOING?
OH, HEY, ROSETTA. I'M DOING MY JOB, OF COURSE!
UM... SINCE WHEN HAVE YOU ACTED LIKE A REAL GARDEN FAIRY?
I KNOW IT MUST SEEM STRANGE!

IT'S TRUE, NORMALLY I'M NOT AS ORGANIZED AS YOU GUYS, AND MY CLOTHES ARE SPLATTERED WITH MUD!
YOU MEAN COVERED WITH MUD!
PAT
PAT

RIGHT, BUT I DECIDED TODAY THAT I'M GOING TO DO IMPECCABLE WORK, AND DO IT WITH STYLE... I WANT TO MAKE THINGS BEAUTIFUL...
WOW!

JUST LIKE YOU!
OH, MY!

WELL, I SURE AM HAPPY TO HEAR YOU SAY THAT, ROSEBUD!

AFTER ALL, YOU COULDN'T CHOOSE A BETTER ROLE MODEL! HEE, HEE!

WELL, I'M OFF TO WORK!
BRAVO! YOU'VE DONE A GREAT JOB ON THIS *APPLE!*

ITS PEEL IS SO RED AND *SMOO--*

GASP! A HOLE!
OOPS!

HOW COULD YOU HAVE OVERLOOKED IT?
UM... ACTUALLY...

DON'T WORRY! I'LL TEACH YOU HOW TO COVER IT UP!
!

WAIT! THERE'S NO NEED!
ARE YOU KIDDING?!
ALL IT TAKES IS A PINCH OF PIXIE DUST AND...
A WORM!
POP
UM, I FORGOT TO TELL YOU... THIS APPLE IS THE HOME OF MY GOOD FRIEND!
SIGH! NOW I UNDERSTAND ALL THAT SPECIAL ATTENTION!
CHLOE WILL NEVER CHANGE... BUT DEEP DOWN THAT'S WHAT MAKES HER UNIQUE!
THE END

THE BRIGHTEST OF THEM ALL

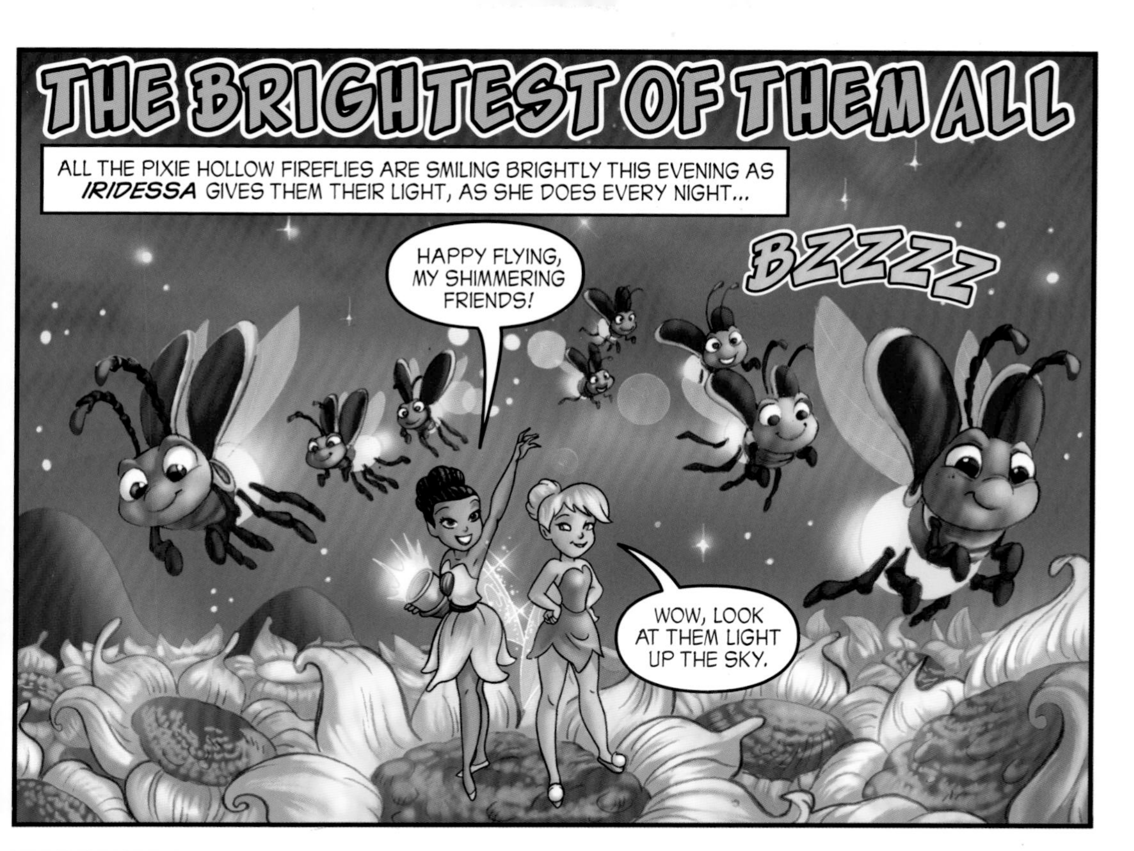

THE FIREFLY POINTS AT THE BRIGHTEST STAR IN THE SKY...
YOU WANT TO BE BRIGHTER?
BZZ

HERE'S SOME MORE LIGHT FOR YOU, BUT DON'T TELL THE OTHERS.

DO YOU THINK SHE'S *HAPPY* NOW?
SOMETHING TELLS ME *SHE ISN'T!*
SIGH

I THINK SHE'S *JEALOUS* OF THAT STAR!
OF THE STAR?! WHY WOULD SHE BE JEALOUS OF A STAR?

BECAUSE SHE THINKS IT'S ANOTHER *FIREFLY* AND DOESN'T UNDERSTAND WHY SHE CAN'T BE JUST AS BRIGHT!

BUT THERE IS NO WAY I CAN MAKE HER SHINE THAT MUCH!
I'VE GOT AN IDEA!

TINKER BELL FLIES OFF AND COMES BACK IN A WINGBEAT WITH...
SILVERMIST?!
SHE CAN HELP US!

SILVERMIST MOVES A LITTLE CLOUD TOWARD THE STAR...
C'MON! A LITTLE FARTHER!

AND DIMS THE STARLIGHT...
WOW! LET'S HOPE IT WORKS...
LOOKS LIKE IT DID! TEE HEE!

PLLLTT
SHE'S ALREADY GETTING BACK AT THE STAR!
HA, HA!
GULP!

SEE? NOW *YOU'RE* BRIGHTER!

OH! THANK YOU!
SMACK

FINALLY, THE FIREFLY GOES OFF TO JOIN HER FRIENDS...
YOU WERE *FLITTERIFIC,* SILVERMIST!
YEAH, WE COULDN'T HAVE DONE IT WITHOUT YOU!
LET'S JUST HOPE THE STAR ISN'T OFFENDED! *HA, HA!*
THE END

A KIND GESTURE OR A NUTTY GESTURE?

WELL, THEN, LET ME HELP YOU!
GASP! ... WHAT ARE YOU DOING?
POFFF
POFFF
I'M HELPING YOU FINISH FASTER!
POFFF
THIS WAY YOU CAN RIPEN THE– OOPS!
SPLOOSH
I BET YOU WERE GOING TO SAY HAZELNUTS, RIGHT?!
THOSE LITTLE NUTS CAN'T WAIT TO BE RIPE! YOU SHOULD MAKE THEM HAPPY!
SIGH ... OH, ALL RIGHT!

AND SO...
SO TELL ME! WHY ARE YOU SO INTERESTED IN THE HAZELNUTS?
WELL, UM... I THINK THEY'RE A LOT PRETTIER WHEN THEY'RE RIPE!
PRETTIER?!
YEAH! BESIDES, WHEN THEY'RE STILL GREEN YOU CAN'T TELL THEM APART FROM THE LEAVES!
ROSETTA DOESN'T REALLY BELIEVE HER, BUT SHE GETS TO WORK ANYWAY...
HMMM! FAWN'S ACTING SO STRANGE TODAY...
PLINN
BESIDES, WHATEVER IT TAKES TO PREVENT FAWN FROM "HELPING OUT" WITH ANY MORE INNOCENT PUMPKINS.
THERE ALL DONE! HAPPY NOW?!
HURRAY! AT LAST, I CAN CALL THEM!
TWEET!

MIND TELLING ME WHO YOU JUST CALLED?!
WITH PLEASURE! TAKE A LOOK DOWN THERE!

RUSTLE
PLINK
PLINK
WELCOME, FRIENDS! HELP YOURSELVES!
GULP!

I PROMISED THEM A SPECIAL SNACK, AND THANKS TO YOU I DIDN'T LET THEM DOWN!
YOU'RE SOMETHING ELSE! HA HA!
SQUEAK
SQUEAK
THE END

DAY AND NIGHT

DON'T BE AFRAID, TINK! IT'S JUST A SOLAR ECLIPSE!
E-ECLIPSE? WHAT'S THAT, IRIDESSA?

IT'S QUITE A RARE ASTRONOMICAL PHENOMENON!

THE MOON IS COVERING UP THE SUN! IT WON'T LAST LONG... WE ARE QUITE LUCKY TO EXPERIENCE SUCH AN EVENT.

EVEN THE ANIMALS IN THE WOODS THINK NIGHT HAS FALLEN!

WELL, FAWN, I HOPE IT ENDS SOON! I WANTED TO HAVE A PICNIC! AND I DON'T LIKE ALL THIS DARKNESS!
BUT IT'S SO MAGICAL!
LOOK! THE SUN'S ALREADY PEEKING OUT!

THE ECLIPSE IS OVER! LET THERE BE LIGHT...
HOORAY! THE SUNSHINE'S BACK!

IT'S NICE TO SEE THE WOODS RETURN TO LIFE!
ONE THING AMAZING ABOUT THAT ECLIPSE IS THAT IT MADE ME APPRECIATE THE SUN EVEN MORE!

I TOLD YOU SO! EVERYTHING'S BACK TO NORMAL! NOW LET'S ENJOY OUR PICNIC.

GULP! LOOKS LIKE SOMEONE ELSE ALSO ENJOYED THE ECLIPSE, HEE HEE.

THAT BIG-EATER, CHEESE, TOOK ADVANTAGE OF THE DARKNESS TO GOBBLE UP ALL OUR PICNIC FOOD!
SQUEAK!
HA! HA! HA!
THE END

WATCH OUT FOR PAPERCUTZ

Welcome to the thirteenth, teamwork-filled DISNEY FAIRIES graphic novel from Papercutz, those competitive kids, dedicated to publishing great graphic novels for all ages! I'm Jim Salicrup, the Editor-in-Chief and refreshment vendor at the Pixie Hollow Games.

Hey, did you know the original Olympic Games began in Ancient Greece back around 776BC in Olympia? In fact, they were held in honor of Zeus, the head of the Greek gods. They even gave the Olympics a mythological origin! So, maybe the Pixie Hollow Games aren't all that far-fetched? For a peek at the origins of the Olympic Games, may I suggest checking out GERONIMO STILTON #10 "Geronimo Stilton Saves the Olympics"? Now, despite Geronimo being a time-traveling mouse and the editor-in-chief of *The Rodent's Gazette*, he does tend to bring back solid, fact-filled information.

But fairies, humans, and mice aren't the only lovable creatures to compete in such major sports competitions! As anyone who has a copy of THE SMURFS #11 "The Smurf Olympics" will tell you, those little blue guys are awesome competitors. Although, come to think of it, we don't recall the Smurfette entering any of the games. Do you suppose she's a little like Rosetta—afraid to get down and dirty? Wanting to remain beautiful at all times? If that's the case, and if you too prefer to stay pretty and not slide though slug slime, you may be interested in the newest graphic novel series from Papercutz: STARDOLL! It's all about fun and fashion, and looking your very best, based on the popular website! On the next few pages, we offer a very short excerpt from STARDOLL #1 "Secrets & Dreams," by JayJay Jackson, writer and artist. In fact, JayJay said that writing, drawing, lettering, and designing an entire graphic novel all by herself was a dream come true for her! Well, we know all about dreams coming true around here! After all, we know that almost anything's possible if you just keep believing in "faith, trust, and pixie dust"!

Thanks,

STAY IN TOUCH!

EMAIL:	salicrup@papercutz.com
WEB:	www.papercutz.com
TWITTER:	@papercutzgn
FACEBOOK:	PAPERCUTZGRAPHICNOVELS
REGULAR MAIL:	Papercutz, 160 Broadway, Suite 700, East Wing, New York, NY 10038

Exclusive Excerpt of STARDOLL #1 "Secrets & Dreams"...

I CAN'T AFFORD ANYTHING. MY DAD TOTALLY REFUSED TO GIVE ME A CREDIT CARD. HE SAYS HE WANTS ME TO REMEMBER WHERE I CAME FROM.
CASE OF THE "ROOTS," HUH?
OH, YEAH.
YOU SHOULD TELL HIM YOU NEED IT FOR SCHOOL. HE WOULDN'T KNOW WHAT YOU NEED FOR SUPPLIES, FABRICS AND STUFF. PLUS ALL THE FASHION RESEARCH... MAGAZINES, BOOKS.
THAT'S A GREAT IDEA. YOU KNOW, YOU'RE PRETTY DEVIOUS.
I'M A TEENAGER.
MY BROTHER, KALLEN, AND HIS FRIEND, SEBASTIAN, ARE ON THEIR WAY. THEY'VE BEEN WORKING ON SOME TOP SECRET PROJECT. SO YOU KNOW THAT'S GOING TO BE TROUBLE. AS USUAL.
HEY, HEY, EVERYBODY! YOU ARE ALL CHOSEN TO STAR IN THE PREMIERE EPISODE OF KALLENATION! NO AUTOGRAPHS, PLEASE.
THE CROWD GOES WILD!
SEBASTIAN, STOP FILMING! WHAT THE HECK ARE YOU TWO DOING?

WE'RE MAKING OUR OWN REALTY SHOW! AND YOU GUYS ARE IN IT!
DON'T YOU GET ENOUGH OF THAT STUFF? IT'S ALL YOU EVER WATCH!
I'M NOT DRESSED FOR BEING FILMED!
NONE OF US HAVE OUR MAKEUP DONE!

I'VE DECIDED THAT'S WHAT I WANT TO BE! A REALITY TV STAR. I AUDITIONED BUT THEY NEVER CALLED, SO I'M TIRED OF WAITING. WE'RE GOING TO DO IT OURSELVES.
WE GOT OUR OWN YOOSCREEN CHANNEL!

ARE YOU KIDDING ME?
YOU CAN'T DO THIS.
OH, WHAT ARE YOU SO WORRIED ABOUT? C'MON, SEBASTIAN, LETS FILM THE INTRODUCTIONS.

THIS IS MY BEAUTIFUL SISTER, KAYA... WELL, MOST OF THE TIME SHE'S BEAUTIFUL. NOT RIGHT NOW.
KALLEN! CUT IT OUT!

AND THESE ARE HER FRIENDS...
UH...
I'M NOT TOO SURE THIS IS A GOOD IDEA.
I'M PRETTY SURE IT'S NOT. YOU DIDN'T ASK US IF WE WANTED TO BE IN IT. ARE YOU EVEN GETTING MODEL RELEASES?
IT SOUNDS KIND OF FUN. WHAT'S THE SHOW GOING TO BE ABOUT?